K is for Kobe,
A is for Abby
and
Alex !!
Keep reading and
Creating!

A work of imagination,
a hand-made labor of love,
this book is for readers
ages 2 and well above!

"For Maya, Aliya, and Pippa of course...
and for Bob, who brings the X-factor!"

- J. L.

"For Hayden, who brings laughter,
inspiration, and lives the dream every day."

- T. P.

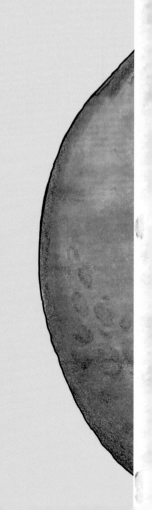

J IS FOR JITTERBUG
A Fanciful Animal Alphabet

a book in poetry by
Jen Laffler

with illustrations by
Tony Perrin

a Just a little Genius ink. production

A a
IS FOR
ANT
AND
ANTEATER

Look out in the dirt - it's an ANTEATER alert!

Clever queen has a plan so no ANT will get hurt!

Worker ANTS build a tunnel - the job's almost done -

Now ANTEATER slurps *trash* with its long, sticky tongue!

Bb
IS FOR
BUTTERFLY

They're delicate creatures, yet surprisingly tough

Soaring high in the sky on a wing and a puff –

Sipping nectar from flowers, at home in the trees,

BUTTERFLIES ride the breeze to wherever they please!

C c

IS FOR

CAT

AND

CANARY

For some
little birds,
kitty CATs
can be scary

But that's not
how it is
for rock star
CANARIES!

'Cause the CAT
kickin' back
in a hammock
on this page

Is just chillin'
to the tune of
CANARIES
on stage!

Dd
IS FOR
DUCK
AND
DUCK
BILLED
PLATYPUS

In finest of
feathers –
see 'em all
dressed up?

PLATYPUS
eats a fancy
dinner with
a DUCK!

PLATYPUS
says, "Are you
kidding?
Am I reading
this right?!

These worms,
bugs and grass
cost a fortune
tonight!"

E e

IS FOR

E L E P H A N T

ELEPHANT's
one cool customer
to run into
at the pump

He doesn't need
a hand – he fills
his tank up
with his trunk!

ELEPHANT
waves a
big grey ear
and makes a
mouseling's day

Then he'll
somehow squeeze
into his truck,
and drive away!

Ff

IS FOR

FLYING FISH

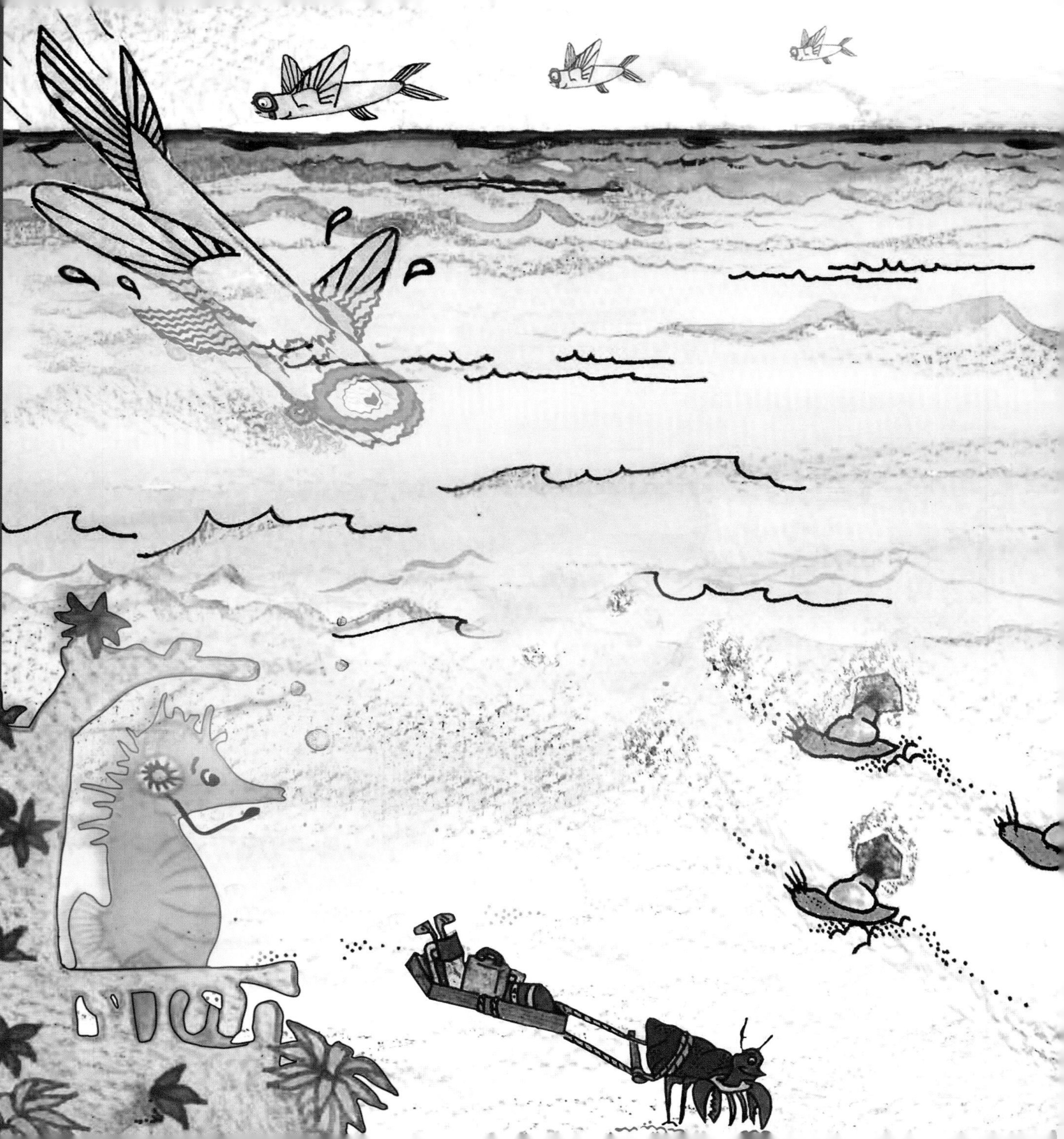

With turbo-
charged tails
and fins
just like sails

FLYING FISH
jet away,
the wind in
their scales

And when the
flight's over,
splashing down
with a dunk,

They land
underwater
with a fishy
KER-PLUNK!

G g

IS FOR

GIRAFFE

Super-long
necks help
them reach
tree-top food

Everywhere
GIRAFFES go,
they bring
the best view!

At a cool
canary concert,
in the forest
canopy

It's great being
a GIRAFFE -
it's easy
to see!

HIPPOS are big, proud, powerful dudes

They're tough, but graceful, with huge attitudes!

They can get really grumpy, so don't mess with their food –

Sumo-wrestling HIPPOS are already in a mood!

I i

IS FOR

IBEX

High in
icy peaks,
IBEX are
looking down

Into a scene
of skiiers in a
winter white
playground

IBEX don't need
skis or rope
to help them
get around -

They can climb
tall mountains,
in leaps and
big bold
bounds!

J j

IS FOR

JITTERBUG

Flitting, flipping, double-dare dipping: JITTERBUGS cut a rug!

Smiling faces, quick-stepping feet - now this is no typical bug!

JITTERBUG's a special species that rocks, hip-hops, and swings

You can JITTERBUG too, it's true! - just dance like you have wings!

K k
IS FOR

KANGAROO

L l
IS FOR
LEMMING

LEMMING's a
famous, fearless
jumper

Willing to give
a tall cliff a
try –

But did you know
LEMMING
is also a fine
swimmer?

Way to go,
LEMMING –
now go and
get dry!

M m
IS FOR

MOOSE

N *n*
IS FOR
NEWT

NEWT's
at home on
slippery
rocks

Special slime
on his skin
keeps him safe
from the fox

Near a stream,
a rushing river,
or little lake
perhaps -

NEWT
basks in
the sunshine,
or enjoys a
nice NEWT
nap!

HOME NEWT HOME

Oo IS FOR OCTOPUS

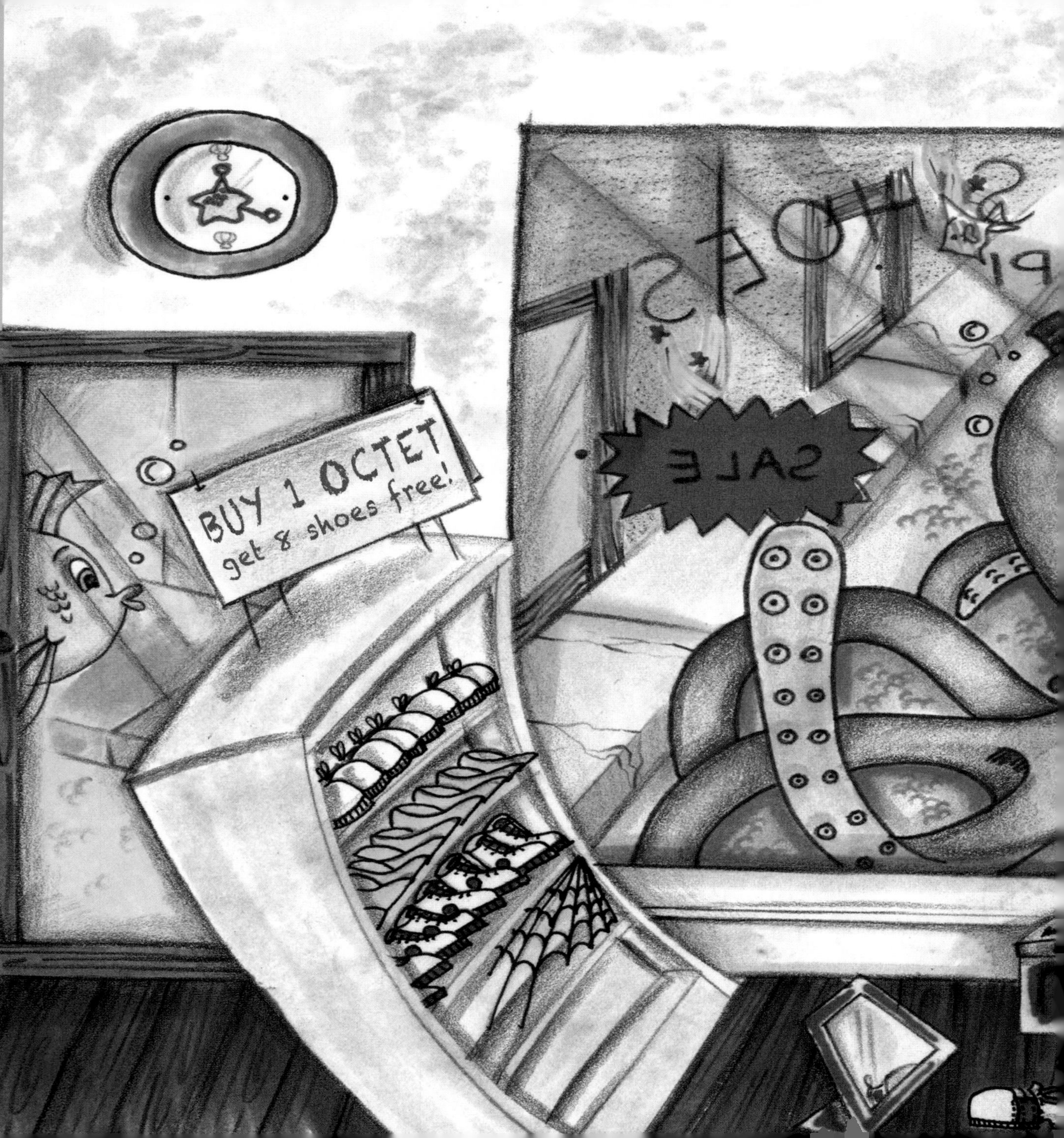

Welcome to a shop for OCTOPUS shoes!

But why do our undersea friends look so blue?

I guess a shoe store's just not much of a treat

When you've got eight legs, but you don't have feet!

P p
IS FOR
P A N D A

PLATES

When it comes to finding food to eat

A bamboo buffet's the perfect PANDA treat!

"Keep the green stuff coming!", pampered PANDAS say

Their plates are packed with veggies, and they like it that way!

Q q IS FOR QUAIL

QUAIL's
on a quest
for sweet,
juicy seeds

Quietly picking
and pecking
in grasses
and reeds

QUAIL set
out in style,
with a quick,
springy step

And a
quirky black
feather held
high in each
cap.

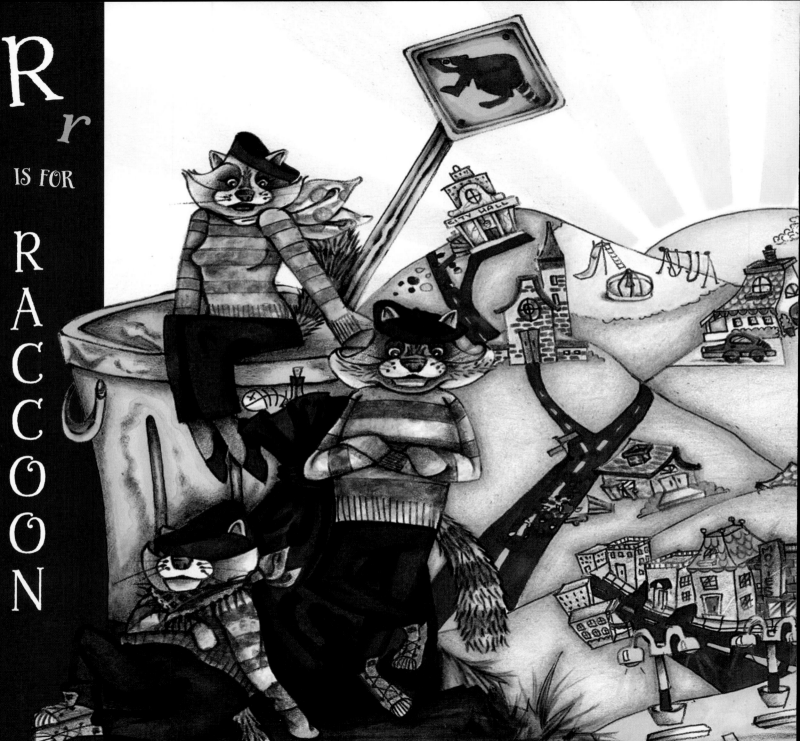

R r
IS FOR
RACCOON

RACCOON'S
up all night,
sneaking and
exploring

Digging through
trash cans
while humans
are snoring

And when
the sun rises,
RACCOON
goes to sleep

As people
wake up to
leftovers
in the street!

S s IS FOR

SLUG

Some silly kid
brought a
SLUG family
in -

Now they're
out of their
cage and
taking a spin!

Outside,
of course, is
where dancing
SLUGS belong

'Cause slime
on your
parents' rug -
it's just *wrong!*

Tt
IS FOR
TERRAPIN

With a duck of his head and shrug of his shoulders

TERRAPIN transforms into a big old boulder!

"Ahoy there, matey! You've discovered new land!

Ye didn't get here first though — there be critters where ye stand!"

U u
IS FOR
UNICORN

Fleet of foot,
coat of white,
horn glowing
light

UNICORN
shines like
a star in
the night

A mythical
creature?
A friend
from afar?

What you
believe is as
unique as
you are.

A thriller
is playing at
the drive-in
tonight!

VIPER's hisses
are vicious, but
mighty mouse'll
make it right!

(You know if I
were a mouse,
I'd stay safe
in my car

Or go grab some
little vittles
from the mouse
snack bar!)

W
w
IS FOR
WHALE

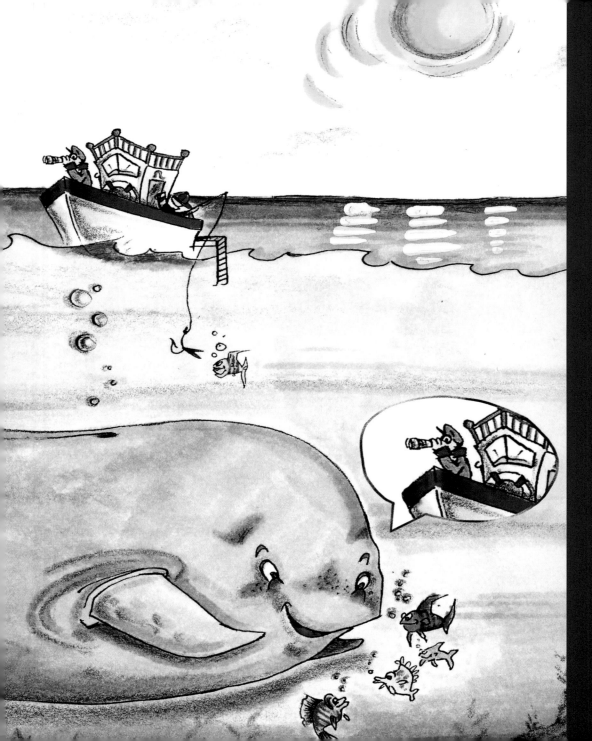

If you spot a spout when you're out at sea,

It might be a WHALE, coming up to breathe!

So keep a good lookout when you're out for a sail

Just catch sight of one, you'll have a WHALE of a tale!

X x

IS FOR

XIAMONGER

At night time when children lie snug in their beds

But instead of tidying up, put stuff underneath instead...

XIAMONGER emerges from out of thin air!

It's said his eyes gleam with a mischievous glare

And his body is covered with white bushy hair

And although he's never been photographed –

You can always tell he's been there:

XIAMONGER takes mess, just a little mess, and spreads it everywhere!

He digs in your drawers
and splits up your socks

He inside-outs your
undies, and upside-downs
your blocks!

He flips through your
books without saving
your page

He'll even let your pet
rats out of their cage!

He mixes up clean and
dirty clothes – such a
funky sense of style –

And the rest he flings
all 'round the room,
from his perch atop a
great big your-things pile!

So kids, you should beware,
lest a XIAMONGER's
lying in wait:

Clean up your mess really,
when it's time to go to bed,
Or find MEGA-MESS
when you awake!

Birds love
to coo, sing,
chatter,
and such

Our friend
Yessika YAK?
Not so much.

'Cause you can
cluck or *hoo-hoo*
or even *quackity-
quack-quack*

But you can't
expect YAK
to yack-ity
yack back!

AND

Z z

IS FOR

ZEBRA

In racing
stripes of white
and black

See ZEBRAS
zoom around
the track!

It's close -
a photo finish!
Can you tell
which one wins?

From ANT to
ZEBRA, what
a wild ride
it's been...

Come back soon,
Read us again!

THE END

For information go to www.justalittlegenius.com

Concept, poetry, book design & production by Jen Laffler / **JALG, Ink**.
Hand-rendered mixed-media illustrations by Tony Perrin.
Graphic design and technical expertise by Dave Warren of DB Creative, Inc.
Proofreading and writerly helpfulness rendered by Karen Russell of Fresh Ink.
Practically professional encouragement provided by Rosalie Cushman.

ISBN: 978-0-615-45686-7

Fonts (Liam and Honeybee) by Laura Worthington.
Printed in Visalia, CA by Jostens, Inc.

First Edition

Jen and Tony, friends for years and years,
proud author and illustrator of
J is for JITTERBUG: A Fanciful Animal Alphabet

Imagine the amazing things
you and your friends will do!